3 4028 06603 2443
HARRIS COUNTY PUBLIC LIBRARY

YA 741.
Serenit

D0651322

$9.99
ocn156812032
04/01/2008

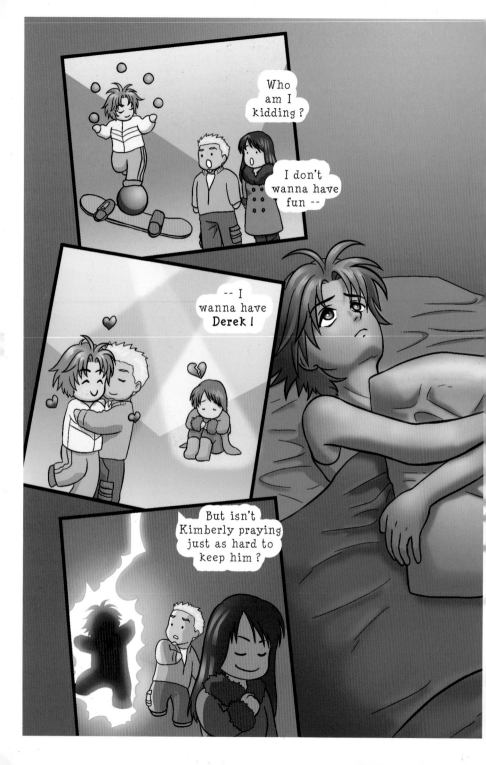

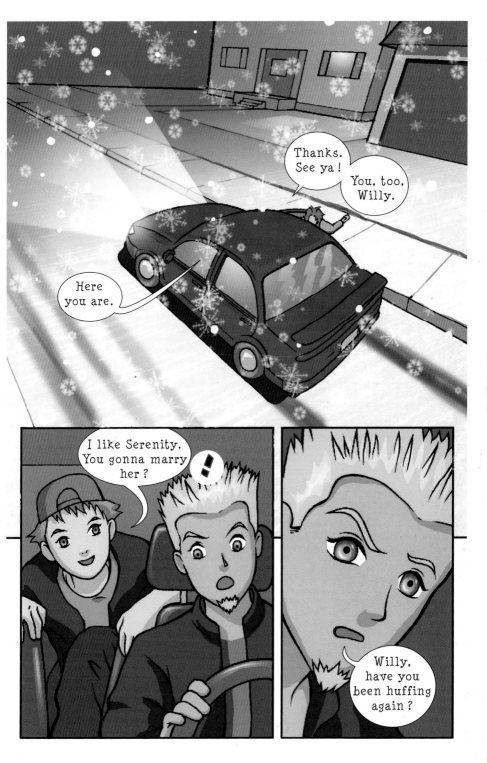

* See SERENITY: Stepping Out

See **Serenity** #1

Tim, would you please read our study verse?

Matthew 5:43-44

"You have heard that it was said, 'Love your neighbor and hate your enemies.' But I say to you, love your enemies. Pray for those who hurt you..."

New Century Version (NCV)

Say wha -- ? Huh? Why be nice to somebody who **hates** you?

Doesn't it bug you when people dis your puns?

It's just funnin'.

But clipping me wasn't! You really ticked me off!

???

Life's a beach --
come and play!

"INSANELY UNIQUE !"
-- MangaPunk.com

GOOFYFOOT GURL

You can find
anything on a beach
-- especially FUN
and ROMANCE !

Making her splash in Summer 2007 !

Created by Realbuzz Studios
Published by Thomas Nelson
Find out more at
www.RealbuzzStudios.com

Wanna see ?
Turn the page for a
SPECIAL SNEAK
PREVIEW !!!

GOOFYFOOT GURL
hitting the beach this September!

THE revolve TOUR

ALL NEW EVENT for Teen Girls
PRESENTED BY WOMEN OF FAITH

Hawk Nelson

Natalie Grant

KJ-52

Max & Jenna Lucado

Ayiesha Woods

Chad Eastham

Kimiko Soldati

We're Coming to a City Near You!
TOUR DATES

Columbus, OH
September 14 - 15, 2007

Dallas, TX
September 21 - 22, 2007

Hartford, CT
September 28 - 29, 2007

St. Louis, MO
October 5 - 6. 2007

Anaheim, CA
October 12 - 13, 2007

Sacramento, CA
October 19 - 20, 2007

Philadelphia, PA
November 2 - 3, 2007

Minneapolis, MN
November 9 - 10, 2007

Portland, OR
November 16 - 17, 2007

Atlanta, GA
November 30 - Dec. 1, 2007

Orlando, FL
January 25 - 26, 2008

Charlotte, NC
February 1 - 2, 2008

Denver, CO
February 15 - 16, 2008

Houston, TX
February 22 - 23, 2008

Download **Preview Video** Online

To register by phone, call 877-9-REVOLVE
or online at REVOLVETOUR.COM

Dates, locations and guests are subject to change.
The Revolve Tour is produced by Women of Faith, Inc. Women of Faith is a ministry division of Thomas Nelson Publishers.

Harris County Public Library
Houston, Texas

Serenity

Created by Realbuzz Studios, Inc.
Min Kwon, Primary Artist

Serenity throws a big wet sloppy one out to:
Everyone who helped us get on the CBA bestseller list!

Smack!

Luv U Guyz !!!

©&TM 2007 by Realbuzz Studios   ISBN 1-59554-387-2
www.Realbuzz Studios.com
www.SerenityBuzz.com

All rights reserved. No part of this publication may be reproduced or transmitted for commercial purposes, except for brief quotations in printed reviews, without written permission of the publisher.

This book is a work of fiction. Names, characters, places, and incidents are either products of the author's imagination or used fictitiously. Any similarity to actual people, organizations, and/or events is purely coincidental.

Published by Thomas Nelson, Inc. Nashville, TN 37214 www.thomasnelson.com

Library of Congress Cataloguing-in-Publication Data
Applied For

Scripture quotations marked NCV are taken from
The HOLY BIBLE, New Century VERSION®. NCV®.
Copyright © 2001 by Nelson Bibles.
Used by permission of Thomas Nelson. All rights reserved.

Printed in Singapore.
5 4 3 2 1